MORE
SCARY STORIES
TO TELL
IN THE DARK

ALSO BY
ALVIN SCHWARTZ

MORE SCARY STORIES TO TELL IN THE DARK

COLLECTED FROM FOLKLORE
AND RETOLD BY
ALVIN SCHWARTZ

ILLUSTRATED BY
BRETT HELQUIST

HARPER
An Imprint of HarperCollinsPublishers

More Scary Stories to Tell in the Dark
Text copyright © 1984 by Alvin Schwartz
Illustrations © 2010 by Brett Helquist
All rights reserved. Printed in the United States of America. No part of this book
may be used or reproduced in any manner whatsoever without written permission
except in the case of brief quotations embodied in critical articles and reviews. For
information address HarperCollins Children's Books, a division of HarperCollins
Publishers, 195 Broadway, New York, NY 10007.
www.harpercollinschildrens.com

Library of Congress catalog card number: 2010922248
ISBN 978-0-06-083521-7 (trade bdg.)
ISBN 978-0-06-083522-4 (pbk.)
Typography by Torborg Davern
14 15 16   LP/RRDH   10 9 8 7 6 5
❖
First Harper Trophy edition, 1986
Reillustrated Harper Trophy edition, 2010

"Something Was Wrong" and "The Bed by the Window" are adapted from the untitled stories on pages 275–76 and 288–89 of *Try and Stop Me* by Bennett Cerf. Copyright © 1944 by Bennett Cerf, renewal copyright © 1971 by Mrs. Bennett Cerf, Christopher Cerf, and Jonathan Cerf. Reprinted by permission of Simon & Schuster, Inc.
"The Cat in a Shopping Bag" is adapted from untitled texts on pages 108 and 109 of *The Vanishing Hitchhiker: American Urban Legends and Their Meanings* by Jan Harold Brunvand, by permission of W.W. Norton & Company, Inc. Copyright © 1981 by Jan Harold Brunvand.

CONTENTS

To Lauren
—A. S.

HOO-HA'S

These scary stories will take you on a strange and fearsome journey, where darkness or fog or mist or the sound of a person screaming or a dog howling turns ordinary places into nightmarish places, where nothing is what you expect.

People have been telling scary stories for as long as anyone knows. From the first, they were tales of supernatural creatures that people feared would harm them—bogeymen, monsters, demons, ghosts, and evil spirits lurking in the dark, waiting for a chance to strike.

We still tell stories about creatures we fear, but not all of them are about bogeymen and demons. Quite a few are about living people. You'll meet some of them—a fat and jolly butcher, a friendly girl who plays a drum, a neighbor, and others who, at best, are not to be trusted.

Scary stories of this kind often have a serious

purpose. They may warn young people of dangers that await them when they set out in the world on their own.

But for the most part, we tell scary stories to have fun. We turn out the lights, or we leave just a candle burning. Then we sit close together and tell the scariest stories we know. Often these include some that have been passed down over hundreds of years.

If a story is scary enough, your flesh begins to creep. You get a shivery, shaky, screamy feeling. You imagine hearing and seeing things. You hold your breath as you wait to learn how it all ends. If something startling happens, everyone GASPS! or JUMPS! or SCREAMS!

Some people call those shivery, shaky, screamy feelings the "heebee jeebies" or the "screaming meemies." The poet T. S. Eliot called them the "hoo-ha's."

You'd better read the stories in this book while you are still feeling brave and *before* it gets dark. *Then,* when the moon is up, tell them to your friends and relatives. You'll probably give them the "hoo-ha's." But they'll have fun, and so will you.

Princeton, New Jersey   ALVIN SCHWARTZ

WHEN SHE SAW HIM, SHE SCREAMED AND RAN

*This chapter is filled with ghost stories.
In one, a man has just become a ghost,
but doesn't know it yet. In another,
a pirate ship and crew return from a watery
grave. And there are other frightful events.*

SOMETHING
WAS WRONG

One morning John Sullivan found himself walking along a street downtown. He could not explain what he was doing there, or how he got there, or where he had been earlier. He didn't even know what time it was.

He saw a woman walking toward him and stopped her. "I'm afraid I forgot my watch," he said, and smiled. "Can you tell me the time?" When she saw him, she screamed and ran.

Then John Sullivan noticed that other people were afraid of him. When they saw him coming, they flattened themselves against a building, or ran across the street to stay out of his way.

"There must be something wrong with me," John Sullivan thought. "I'd better go home."

He hailed a taxi, but the driver took one look at him and sped away.

John Sullivan did not understand what was going on, and it scared him. "Maybe somebody at home can come and get me," he thought. He found a telephone and called his wife, but a voice he did not recognize answered.

"Is Mrs. Sullivan there?" he asked.

"No, she is at a funeral," the voice said. "Mr. Sullivan was killed yesterday in an accident downtown."

THE WRECK

Fred and Jeanne went to the same high school, but they met for the first time at the Christmas dance. Fred had come by himself, and so had Jeanne. Soon Fred decided that Jeanne was one of the nicest girls he had ever met. They danced together most of the evening.

At eleven o'clock Jeanne said, "I have to leave now. Can you give me a ride?"

"Sure," he said. "I've got to go home, too."

"I accidentally drove my car into a tree on my way over here," Jeanne said. "I guess I wasn't paying attention."

Fred drove her to the head of Brady Road. It was in a neighborhood he didn't know very well.

"Why don't you drop me off here," Jeanne said. "The road up ahead is in really bad condition. I can walk from here."

Fred stopped the car and held out some tinsel. "Have some," he said. "I got it at the dance."

"Thank you," she said. "I'll put it in my hair," and she did.

"Would you like to go out sometime, to a movie or something?" Fred asked.

"That would be fun," Jeanne said.

After Fred drove off, he realized that he did not know Jeanne's last name or her telephone number. "I'll go back," he thought. "The road can't be that bad."

He drove slowly down Brady Road through a thick woods, but there wasn't a sign of Jeanne. As he came around a curve, he saw the wreckage of a car ahead. It had crashed into a tree and had caught fire. Smoke was still rising from it.

As Fred made his way to the car, he could see someone trapped inside, crushed against the steering column.

It was Jeanne. In her hair was the Christmas tinsel he had given her.

ONE SUNDAY MORNING

Ida always went to the seven o'clock Sunday morning service at her church. Usually she heard the clanging of the church bells while she was eating breakfast. But this morning she heard them while she was still in bed.

"That means I'm late," she thought.

Ida jumped out of bed, quickly dressed and left without eating or looking at the clock. It was still dark outside, but it usually was dark at this time of year. Ida was the only one on the street. The only sounds she heard were the clatter of her shoes on the pavement. "Everybody must already be in church," she thought.

Ida took a short cut through the cemetery, then she quietly slipped into the church and found a seat. The service had already begun.

When she caught her breath, Ida looked around.

The church was filled with people she had never seen before. But the woman next to her did look familiar. Ida smiled at her. "It's Josephine Kerr," she thought. "But she's dead! She died a month ago." Suddenly Ida felt uneasy.

She looked around again. As her eyes began to adjust to the dim light, Ida saw some skeletons in suits and dresses. "This is a service for the dead," Ida thought. "Everybody here is dead, except me."

Ida noticed that some of them were staring at her. They looked angry, as if she had no business there. Josephine Kerr leaned toward her and whispered, "Leave right after the benediction, if you care for your life."

When the service came to an end, the minister gave his blessing. "The Lord bless you and keep you," he said. "The Lord make his face to shine upon you . . ."

Ida grabbed her coat and walked quickly toward the door. When she heard footsteps behind her, she glanced back. Several of the dead were coming toward her. Others were getting up to join them.

"The Lord lift up his countenance to you . . ." the minister went on.

Ida was so frightened she began to run. Out the door she ran, with a pack of shrieking ghosts at her heels.

"Get out!" one of them screamed. Another shouted, "You don't belong here!" and ripped her coat away. As Ida ran through the cemetery, a third grabbed the hat from her head. "Don't come back!" it screamed, and shook its arm at her.

By the time Ida reached the street, the sun was rising, and the dead had disappeared.

"Did this really happen?" Ida asked herself, "or have I been dreaming?"

That afternoon one of Ida's friends brought over her coat and hat, or what was left of them. They had been found in the cemetery, torn to shreds.

SOUNDS

The house was near the beach. It was a big old place where nobody had lived for years. From time to time somebody would force open a window or a door and spend the night there. But never longer.

Three fishermen caught in a storm took shelter there one night. With some dry wood they found inside, they made a fire in the fireplace. They lay down on the floor and tried to get some sleep, but none of them slept that night.

First they heard footsteps upstairs. It sounded like there were several people moving back and forth, back and forth. When one of the fishermen called, "Who's up there?" the footsteps stopped. Then they heard a woman scream. The scream turned into a groan and died away. Blood began to drip from the ceiling into the room where the fishermen huddled. A small red pool formed on the floor and soaked into the wood.

A door upstairs crashed shut, and again the woman screamed. "Not me!" she cried. It sounded as if she was running, her high heels tapping wildly down the hall. "I'll get you!" a man shouted, and the floor shook as he chased her.

Then silence. There wasn't a sound until the man who had shouted began to laugh. Long peals of horrible laughter filled the house. It went on and on until the fishermen thought they would go mad.

When finally it stopped, the fishermen heard someone coming down the stairs dragging something heavy that bumped on each step. They heard him drag it through the front hall and out the front door. The door opened; then it slammed shut. Again, silence.

Suddenly a flash of lightning filled the house with a green blaze of light. A ghastly face stared at the fishermen from the hallway. Then came a crash of thunder. Terrified, they ran out into the storm.

A WEIRD
BLUE LIGHT

Late one night in October, 1864, a Confederate blockade runner slipped by some Union gunboats at the entrance to Galveston Bay in Texas and made it safely to port with its cargo of food and other necessities.

Louis Billings, the master of the small vessel, was getting ready to weigh anchor when he was startled by a shriek from one of the crew.

"A strange, old-fashioned schooner with a big black flag was rushing down at us," Billings said later. "She was afire with a sort of weird, pale-blue light that lighted up every nook and cranny of her.

"The crew was pulling at the ropes and doing other work, and they paid us no attention, didn't even glance our way. They all had ghastly bleeding wounds, but their faces and eyes were those of dead men.

"The man who had shrieked had fallen to his

knees, his teeth chattering as he gasped out a prayer. Overcoming my own terror, that was chilling the very marrow of my bones, I rushed forward, shouting to the others as I ran. Suddenly the schooner vanished before my eyes."

Some say that it was the ghost of Jean Lafitte's pirate ship *Pride* that sank off Galveston Island in 1821 or 1822. She was seen again in 1892 in the same waters with the same crew.

SOMEBODY FELL
FROM ALOFT

I had signed on as an ordinary seaman on the *Falls of Ettrick*, a merchant ship bound for England. The first time I saw that ship, I knew her right away. She was the old *Gertrude Spurshoe*. I had sailed on her years before when she was painted brown and gold. Now she was painted black and had a new name, but it was the same ship for sure.

We had a pretty good crew for that voyage, except

for one hard-looking ticket named McLaren. He was a pretty good seaman, but there was something about him that I didn't trust. He was kind of secretive. Kept mostly to himself.

One day somebody told him that I had worked on the old *Gertrude*. For some reason he got all a-tremble over that. Then I ketched him giving me all of these ugly black looks, as if he was itchin' to knife me in the back. I guessed it had something to do with the *Gertrude*, but I didn't know what.

Well, this one day we was tryin' to work our way through a drippin' black fog. You'd scarcely know we had all the lights on. And it was dead calm. There wasn't a breath of fresh air. The ship just lay there wallowing in a trough, a-rollin' and a-rollin', goin' nowheres.

I was standing my watch around midships, and McLaren was doin' his trick at the wheel. The rest of the crew was scattered around one place and another. It was as quiet as could be.

Then all at once—WHACKO! This thing hits the deck right in front of McLaren! He lets go a screech that turns my blood cold and he falls down in a faint.

The second mate starts yellin' that somebody has fallen from aloft. Layin' out there just forward of the wheel was someone, or something, dressed in oil-skins with blood oozin' out from underneath. The captain ran and fetched a big light from his cabin so we could see who it was.

They kind of straightened him out to get a good look at his face. He was a big, ugly-lookin' devil. But nobody knew who he was or what he was doin' up there. At least nobody was sayin'.

When McLaren came to from his faint, they tried to get somethin' out of him. All he did was jabber away and keep rollin' those big, wild-looking eyes of his.

Everybody was gettin' more and more excited. We all wanted to heave the body overboard as quick as we could. There was somethin' weird about it, as if it wasn't real.

But the captain wasn't so sure about getting rid of it that way. "Could it be a stowaway?" he asked. But the ship was so filled with lumber we were carryin', there was no space where a livin' thing could hide for three weeks, which is how long we had been out. Even if it was a stowaway, what was it doing aloft on such a dirty day? There was no reason for anyone to be up there. There was nothin' to see.

Finally, the captain gave up and told us to heave him overboard. Then nobody would touch him. The mate ordered us to pick him up, but nobody made a move. Then he tried coaxin', but that didn't do any good.

Suddenly that loony McLaren starts yellin', "I handled him once, and I can handle him again!" He picks up the body, and staggers over to the railin' with it. He is just about to throw it overboard when it wraps its two big, long arms around him, and over they go together! Then on the way down, one of them starts laughin' in a horrible way.

The mates are yellin' to launch a boat, but nobody would get into a boat, not on a night like that. We threw a couple of life preservers after them, but everybody knew they wouldn't help. So that was that. Or was it?

The first chance I had to go home after that, I went right over to see old Captain Spurshoe, who was captain when the *Gertrude* was around.

"Well," he says, "one trip these two outlandish men shipped aboard the *Gertrude*. One was McLaren, the other was a really big fella. The big one was always pickin' on McLaren and thumpin' him around. And McLaren was always talkin' about how he would get back at him.

"Well, this wet, dirty night the two of them was up there alone, and the big one come flyin' down, killed himself deader'n a herring.

"McLaren says the foot rope they were using parted and how he almost fell himself. But everybody who saw that rope knew she didn't give away on her own. She had been cut through with a knife.

"After that whenever we came into port, McLaren thought we were goin' to get the police after him, and he'd get pretty scared. But we couldn't prove anything, so we didn't try. In the end, I guess the big fella took care of things in his own way. If he was a ghost that came back, that's what he was—if there be things like ghosts."

THE LITTLE
BLACK DOG

Billy Mansfield said that a little black dog followed him wherever he went. But he was the only one who saw it. So people thought he was kind of crazy. To drive the dog away, Billy was always hollering at it, throwing rocks at it. But the dog always came back.

The first time Billy saw that dog was the day he fought Silas Burton. Billy was just a young man then, but the Burtons and Billy's family had been feuding for years.

When Billy saw Silas riding toward him, he went for his gun and Burton went for his. But Billy fired first. He hit Burton in the back, knocking him from his horse. Burton's horse ran off, and his gun fell where he couldn't reach it.

He lay there on the ground pleading with Billy not to kill him, but Billy killed him anyway. Burton's little black dog was with him when he was shot. The dog kept licking Burton's face, and barking and snarling at Billy. In his anger, Billy killed the dog too.

There wasn't much law enforcement in those days, so Billy wasn't arrested. But all that night he heard Burton's dog outside his cabin, scratching on his door and barking to be let in. "I'm imagining this," Billy said to himself. "I shot that dog. It's dead."

But the next morning Billy *saw* the dog. It was waiting for him outside. From then on there was not a day when he didn't see it. And there wasn't a night when he didn't hear it scratching on his door, barking to be let in.

From then on, Billy was always finding black dog hairs on the sofa, on the floor, in his bed, even in his food. And the house and the yard stank of dog. That's what Billy said.

Whenever somebody told him there wasn't any dog to see, he'd say, "Maybe *you* don't see it, but I do. And I'm not any crazier than you are."

Things went on like that for many years. Then one morning in the middle of the winter the neighbors didn't see any smoke coming out of Billy's chimney. When they went over to check, Billy wasn't there. A day or so later they found his body lying in the snow in a field back of his cabin.

Billy had plenty of enemies, and at first it seemed like somebody might have killed him. But there wasn't a mark on his body. And there weren't any footprints out there, except for Billy's.

The doctor said Billy probably died of old age. But there was something odd about his death. When the neighbors found Billy, there were black dog hairs on his clothes. There were even a few on his face. It smelled like a dog had been out there. Yet no one had seen a dog anywhere.

CLINKITY-CLINK

An old lady got sick and died. She had no family and no close friends. So the neighbors got a gravedigger to dig a grave for her. And they had a coffin made, and they placed it in her living room. As was the tradition, they washed her body and dressed her up in her best clothes and put her in the coffin.

When she died her eyes were wide open, staring at everything and seeing nothing. The neighbors found two old silver dollars on her dresser, and they put them on her eyelids to keep them closed.

They lit candles and sat up with her so that she would not be too lonely on that first night that she was dead. The next morning a preacher came and said a prayer for her. Then everybody went home.

Later the gravedigger arrived to take her to the cemetery and bury her. He stared at the silver dollars on her eyes, and he picked them up. How shiny and smooth they were! How thick and heavy! "They're beautiful," he thought, "just beautiful."

He looked at the dead woman. With her eyes wide open, he felt she was staring at him, watching him hold her coins. It gave him a creepy feeling. He put the coins back on those eyes of hers to keep them closed.

But before he knew it, his hands reached out again and grabbed the coins and stuck them in his pocket. Then he grabbed a hammer and quickly nailed shut the lid on the coffin.

"Now you can't see anything!" he said to her. Then he took her out to the cemetery, and he buried her as fast as he could.

When the gravedigger got home, he put the two silver dollars in a tin box and shook it. The coins made a cheerful rattling sound, but the grave-digger wasn't feeling cheerful. He couldn't forget those eyes looking at him.

When it got dark, a storm came up, and the wind started blowing. It blew all around the house. It came in through the cracks and around the windows, and down the chimney.

BUZ-OOOOOO-O-O-O! it went. *Bizee, bizee,* BUZ-OOOOOO-O-O-O! The fire flared and flickered.

The gravedigger threw some fresh wood on the fire, got into bed, and pulled the blankets up to his chin.

The wind kept blowing. BUZ-OOOOOO-O-O-O! it went. *Bizee, bizee,* BUZ-OOOOOO-O-O-O! The fire flared and flickered and cast evil-looking shadows on the walls.

The gravedigger lay there thinking about the dead woman's eyes staring at him. The wind blew stronger and louder, and the fire flared and flickered, and popped and snapped, and he got more and more scared.

Suddenly he heard another sound. *Clinkity-clink, clinkity-clink,* it went. *Clinkity-clink, clinkity-clink.* It was the silver dollars rattling in the tin box.

"Hey!" the gravedigger shouted. "Who's taking my money?"

But all he heard was the wind blowing, *Bizee, bizee,*

BUZ-OOOOOO-O-O-O! and the flames flaring and flickering, and snapping and popping, and the coins going *clinkity-clink, clinkity-clink*.

He leaped out of bed and chained up the door. Then he hurried back. But his head had barely touched the pillow when he heard, *clinkity-clink, clinkity-clink*.

Then he heard something way off in the distance. It was a voice crying, "Where is my money? Who's got my money? Whoooo? Whoooo?"

And the wind blew *Bizee, bizee,* BUZ-OOOOOO-O-O-O! And the fire flared and flickered and snapped and popped, and the money went *clinkity-clink, clinkity-clink*.

The gravedigger was really scared. He got out of bed again and piled all the furniture against the door, and he put a heavy iron skillet over the tin box. Then he jumped back into bed and covered his head with the blankets.

But the money rattled louder than ever, and way off a voice cried, "Give me my money! Who's got my money! Whoooo? Whoooo?" And the wind blew and the fire flared and flickered and snapped and popped, and the gravedigger shivered and shook and cried, "Oh, Lordy, Lordy!"

Suddenly the front door flew open, and in walked

the ghost of the dead woman with her eyes wide open, staring at everything and seeing nothing. And the wind blew *Bizee, bizee,* BUZ-OOOOOO-O-O-O! and the money went *clinkity-clink, clinkity-clink*, and the fire flared and flickered and snapped and popped, and the ghost of the dead woman cried, "Oh, where is my money? Who's got my money? Whoooo? Whoooo?" And the gravedigger moaned, "Oh, Lordy, Lordy!"

The ghost could hear her money going *clinkity-clink, clinkity-clink*, in the tin box. But her dead eyes couldn't see the box. So she reached out with her arms and tried to find it.

(As you tell the story, stand up with your arms in front of you and begin groping around you.)

The wind went *Bizee, bizee,* BUZ-OOOOOO-O-O-O! and the money rattled, *clinkity-clink, clinkity-clink*! and the fire flared and flickered and snapped and popped, and the gravedigger shivered and shook and moaned, "Oh, Lordy, Lordy!" And the woman cried, "Give me my money! Who's got my money? Whoooo? Whoooo?"

(Now quickly jump at somebody in the audience and scream:)

YOU'VE GOT IT!

SHE WAS SPITTIN' AND YOWLIN' JUST LIKE A CAT

The tales in this chapter
are about an empty trunk,
a neighbor who turns into a cat,
a strange drum,
some very tasty sausages,
and other scary things.

THE BRIDE

The minister's daughter had just gotten married. After the wedding ceremony there was a great feast, with music and dancing and contests and games, even old children's games.

When they got to playing hide-and-seek, the bride decided to hide in her grandfather's trunk up in the attic.

"They'll never find me there," she thought.

As she was climbing into the trunk, the lid came down and cracked her on the head, and she fell unconscious inside. The lid slammed shut and locked.

No one will ever know how long she called for help or how hard she struggled to free herself from that tomb. Everyone in the village searched for her, and they looked almost everywhere. But no one thought of looking in the trunk. After a week her brand-new bridegroom and all the others gave her up for lost.

Years later a maid went up into the attic look-ing for something she needed. "Maybe it is in the trunk," she thought. She opened it—and screamed. There lay the missing bride in her wedding dress, but by then she was only a skeleton.

RINGS ON
HER FINGERS

Daisy Clark had been in a coma for more than a month when the doctor said that she had finally died. She was buried on a cool summer day in a small cemetery about a mile from her home.

"May she always rest in such peace," her husband said.

But she didn't. Late that night a grave robber with

a shovel and a lantern began to dig her up. Since the ground was still soft, he quickly reached the coffin and got it open.

His hunch was right. Daisy had been buried wearing two valuable rings—a wedding ring with a diamond in it, and a ring with a ruby that glowed as if it were alive.

The thief got down on his knees and reached into the coffin to get the rings. But they were stuck fast on her fingers. So he decided that the only way to get them was to cut off her fingers with a knife.

But when he cut into the finger with the wedding ring, it began to bleed, and Daisy Clark began to stir. Suddenly she sat up! Terrified, the thief scrambled to his feet. He accidentally kicked over the lantern, and the light went out.

He could hear Daisy climb out of her grave. As she moved past him in the dark, he stood there frozen with fear, clutching the knife in his hand.

When Daisy saw him, she pulled her shroud around her and asked, "Who are you?" When the grave robber heard this "corpse" speak, he ran! Daisy shrugged her shoulders and walked on, and never once looked back.

But in his fear and confusion, the thief fled in the wrong direction. He pitched headlong into her grave, fell on the knife, and stabbed himself. While Daisy walked home, the thief bled to death.

THE DRUM

Once there were two sisters. Dolores was seven, and Sandra was five. They lived in a small house in the country with their mother and their baby brother, Arthur. Their father was a seaman and was away on a long voyage.

One day Dolores and Sandra were running across a field near their house when they met a gypsy girl playing a drum. Her family was camping in the field for a few days.

As the girl played, a little mechanical man and woman came out of the drum and danced. Dolores and Sandra had never seen such a drum, and they begged the girl to give it to them.

She looked at them and laughed. "I will give it to you," she said, "but only if you are really bad. Come back tomorrow and tell me how bad you were, and I will see."

As soon as the two sisters got home, they started shouting, which was against the rules in their house.

Then they wrote all over the walls with their crayons. At supper, they spilled their food. And when it was time for bed, they wouldn't go. They did everything they could think of to upset their mother. They were really bad.

Early the next morning, they hurried off to find the gypsy girl. "We were really bad yesterday," they told her, "so please give us the drum."

But when they told her what they had done, the gypsy girl laughed.

"Oh, you must be much worse than *that* if I am to give you the drum," she said.

As soon as Dolores and Sandra got home, they pulled up all the flowers in the garden. They let the pig out, and chased it away. They tore their clothes. They sloshed in the mud. They were a lot worse than the day before.

"If you do not stop," their mother said, "I will go away and take Arthur with me. And you will get a new mother with glass eyes and a wooden tail."

That scared Dolores and Sandra. They loved their mother, and they loved Arthur. They could not imagine being without them, and they began to cry.

"I don't want to leave you," their mother said. "But unless you change your behavior, I will have to leave you."

"We'll be good," the girls promised. Yet they did not really believe that their mother would go away.

"She is just trying to scare us," Dolores said later.

"We'll get the drum tomorrow," said Sandra. "Then we'll be good again."

Early the next morning, they rushed off to find the gypsy girl. When they found her, she was playing the drum again, and the little man and woman were dancing.

They told the gypsy girl how bad they had been the day before. "That must be bad enough to get the drum," they said.

"Oh, no," said the gypsy girl. "You must be *much* worse than that."

"But we promised our mother to be good from now on," said the girls.

"If you really want the drum," said the gypsy girl, "you must be much worse."

"It's only for one more day," Dolores told Sandra. "Then we will have the drum."

"I hope you're right," Sandra said.

As soon as they got home, they beat the dog with a stick. They broke the dishes. They tore their clothes to pieces. They spanked their baby brother Arthur.

Their mother began to cry. "You are not keeping

your promise," she said.

"We will be good," said Dolores.

"We promise," said Sandra.

"I can't wait much longer," said their mother. "Please try."

Early the next morning, before their mother was awake, Dolores and Sandra ran to see the gypsy girl. They told her all about the bad things they had done the day before.

"We were horrid," said Sandra.

"We were worse than we have ever been," said Dolores. "Can we have the drum now, please?"

"No," said the gypsy girl. "I never meant to give it to you. It was just a game we were playing. I thought you knew that."

Dolores and Sandra began to cry. They rushed home as quickly as they could. But their mother and Arthur were gone. "They are out shopping," said Dolores. "They'll be back soon." But they were still not back when time for lunch came.

Dolores and Sandra felt lonely and scared. They wandered through the fields the rest of the day. "Maybe they will be home when we get back," said Dolores.

When they got home, they saw through the window that the lamps were lit, and there was a fire in the fireplace. But they did not see their mother and Arthur. Instead, there was their new mother—her glass eyes glistening, her wooden tail thumping on the floor.

THE WINDOW

Margaret and her brothers, Paul and David, shared a small house on top of a hill just outside the village.

It was so warm one summer's night that Margaret could not sleep. She sat up in bed in the darkness of her room watching the moon move across the sky. Suddenly something caught her eye.

She saw two small yellow-green lights moving through the woods near the graveyard at the bottom of the hill. They looked like the eyes of some animal.

But she could not make out what kind of a creature it was.

Soon the creature left the woods and moved up the hill toward the house. For a few minutes, Margaret lost sight of it. Then she saw it coming across the lawn toward her window. It looked something like a man, and yet it didn't.

Margaret was terrified. She wanted to run from her room. But the door was next to her window. She was afraid the creature would see her and break in before she could escape.

When the creature turned and moved in another direction, Margaret rushed to the door. But before she could open the door, it was back. Margaret found herself staring through the window at a shrunken face like that of a mummy. Its yellow-green eyes gleamed like a cat's eyes. She wanted to scream, but she was so frightened that she could not make a sound.

The creature broke the window glass, unlocked the window, and crawled inside. Margaret tried to flee, but the creature caught her. It twisted its long, bony fingers into her hair, pulled back her head, and sank its teeth into her throat.

Margaret screamed, and fainted. When her brothers heard her piercing scream, they rushed to her room. But by the time they got the door unlocked, the creature had fled. Margaret lay on the floor bleeding and unconscious. While Paul tried to stop the bleeding, David chased the creature down the hill toward the graveyard. But soon he lost sight of it.

The police thought it was the work of an escaped lunatic who believed he was a vampire.

When Margaret recovered, her brothers wanted to move to a safer place where it would be harder to break in. But Margaret refused. The creature would never come back. She was sure of that. But just in case, Paul and David began to keep loaded pistols in their rooms.

One night months later, Margaret was awakened by a scratching sound at the window. When she opened her eyes, there was the same shrunken face staring in at her.

That night her brothers heard her cries in time. They chased the creature down the hill, and David shot it in the leg. But the creature managed to scramble over the graveyard wall and disappeared near an old burial vault.

The next day, Margaret and her brothers watched as the sexton of the church opened the burial vault. Inside was a horrifying scene—broken coffins, bones, and rotting flesh were scattered all over the floor.

Only one coffin had not been disturbed. When

the sexton opened it, there lay the creature with the shrunken face that had attacked Margaret. The telltale bullet was in its leg.

They did the only thing they knew of to rid themselves of a vampire. The sexton built a roaring blaze outside the vault, and fed the shrunken body to the flames. They watched the body burn until nothing remained but ashes.

WONDERFUL SAUSAGE

One dark, rainy Saturday afternoon, a fat and jolly butcher named Samuel Blunt had an argument over money with his wife, Eloise. Blunt lost his temper and killed Eloise. Then he ground her up into sausage meat and buried her bones under a big flat rock in the backyard. To keep the murder a secret, he told everyone that she had moved away.

Blunt mixed his new sausage meat with pork, then seasoned it with salt and pepper, added some sage and thyme and a bit of garlic. To give it a special flavor, he smoked it in his smokehouse for a while. He called it "Blunt's Special Sausage."

There was such a demand for this new sausage that Blunt bought the best hogs he could find and started raising his own pork. He also kept a sharp lookout for humans who might make a tasty sausage meat.

One day a nice, plump schoolteacher came into his shop. Blunt grabbed her and ground her up. Another time Blunt's dentist came by. He was a little round man, and into the grinder he went. Then one by one, the children in the neighborhood began to disappear. And so did their kittens and puppies. But no one ever dreamed that Blunt the butcher had anything to do with it.

Things went on that way for years. Then one day Blunt made a big mistake. A fat boy came into the butcher shop. Blunt grabbed him and started to drag him off to the sausage grinder. But the boy broke loose, and ran out of the shop, and Blunt chased after him waving a big butcher knife.

When people saw this, they realized at once what had become of all the missing children and grownups and kittens and puppies. An angry crowd gathered at the butcher shop. No one knows for sure just what happened to Blunt that day. Some say he was fed to his hogs. Others say he was fed to his sausage grinder. But he was never seen again, and neither was his wonderful sausage meat.

THE CAT'S PAW

Somebody was stealing the meat Jed Smith kept in his smokehouse. Every day a ham, or some bacon, or something else was missing. Finally, Jed decided he had to put a stop to it. One night he hid in the smokehouse with his rifle and waited for the thief.

He didn't have to wait long, for soon a black shecat slunk in. She was the biggest cat Jed had ever seen. When she jumped up and pulled down a ham hanging from the ceiling, Jed grabbed his rifle and turned on the lights. But instead of running away, the cat jumped at him. He fired, and shot off one of her paws.

Jed was sure he heard a woman scream right after his gun went off. The cat began tearing around the room, spitting and yowling. Then she ran up the chimney and was gone.

Jed stared at the cat's paw. Only it wasn't a cat's paw anymore. A woman's foot lay wriggling on the floor, all shot up and bloody.

"So it's a witch that's been doing it," he told himself.

Just then one of Jed's neighbors, a fellow named Burdick, came racing down the road to get a doctor. His wife's foot had been shot in an accident, he told Jed. "She's bleedin' pretty bad," he said.

The doctor got to her barely in time. People who were there when it happened said that she was "spittin' and yowlin' just like a cat."

THE VOICE

Ellen had just fallen asleep when she heard a strange voice.

"Ellen," it whispered, "*I am coming up the stairs.*

"*I am on the first step.*

"*Now I am on the second step.*"

Ellen got scared and called her parents, but they didn't hear her, and they didn't come.

Then the voice whispered, "*Ellen, I'm on the top step.*

"Now I'm in the hall.

"Now I'm outside your room."

Then it whispered, *"I'm standing right next to your bed."*

And then,

"I'VE GOT YOU!"

Ellen screamed, and the voice stopped. Her father rushed into the room and turned on the light.

"Somebody is in here!" Ellen said. They looked and looked. Nobody was there.

WHEN I WAKE UP,
EVERYTHING WILL
BE ALL RIGHT

There are scary stories here
about a subway car,
a shopping mall,
and other dangerous places.

"OH, SUSANNAH!"

Susannah and Jane shared a small apartment near the university where they were students. When Susannah got back from the library one night, the lights were out and Jane was asleep. Susannah undressed in the dark and quietly got into bed.

She had almost fallen asleep when she heard someone humming the tune to the song "Oh, Susannah!"

"Jane," she said, "please stop humming; I want to get some sleep."

Jane didn't answer, but the humming stopped, and Susannah fell asleep. She awakened early the next morning—too early, she decided—and was trying to get back to sleep when she heard the humming again.

"Please go back to sleep," she told Jane. "It's too early to get up."

Jane didn't answer, but the humming continued. Susannah became angry. "Cut it out!" she said. "It's not funny." When the humming still did not stop, she lost her temper. She jumped out of bed, pulled the covers off Jane, and screamed. . . .

Jane's head was gone! Somebody had cut off her head!

"I'm having a nightmare," Susannah told herself. "When I wake up, everything will be all right. . . ."

THE MAN IN
THE MIDDLE

It was almost midnight. Sally Truitt had just gotten
on the subway train at Fiftieth Street after visiting
her mother.

"Don't worry," Sally had told her. "The subway is
safe. There is always a policeman on duty." But that
night she didn't see one. Except for her, the subway
car was empty.

At Forty-second Street, three tough-looking men

got on. Two of them were holding up the third, who looked drunk. His head rolled from side to side, and his legs refused to work.

When they got him seated between them, his head came to rest on one of his shoulders. Sally thought he was staring at her. She buried her head in a book and tried not to notice.

At Twenty-eighth Street, one of the men stood up.

"Take it easy, Jim," he said to the man in the middle, and he got off.

At Twenty-third Street, Jim's other friend stood up.

"You'll be fine," he said, and he got off.

Now the only ones left in the car were Jim and Sally. Just then the train went around a sharp curve, and Jim pitched onto the floor at Sally's feet. When she looked down at him, she saw a trickle of blood on the side of his head and, just above it, a bullet hole.

THE CAT IN A
SHOPPING BAG

Mrs. Briggs was driving to the shopping mall to do some last-minute Christmas shopping when she accidentally ran over a cat. She could not bear to leave the corpse on the road for other cars to hit and squash. So she stopped, wrapped the cat in some tissue paper she had with her, and put it in an old shopping bag in the backseat. She would bury it in the backyard when she got home.

At the mall, she parked her car and began walking to one of the stores. She had taken only a few steps when, out of the corner of her eye, she saw a woman reach into the open window of her car and take the shopping bag with the dead cat. Then the woman quickly got into a car nearby and drove away.

Mrs. Briggs ran back to her car and followed the woman. She caught up with her at a diner down the road. She followed her inside and watched the woman slide into a booth and give a waitress her order.

As the woman sat sipping her soda, she reached into Mrs. Briggs' shopping bag. Then she bent down and looked inside. A look of horror crossed her face. She screamed, and fainted.

The waitress called an ambulance. Two attendants carried the woman away on a stretcher. But they left the shopping bag behind. Mrs. Briggs picked up the bag and ran after them.

"This is hers," she called. "It's her Christmas present! She wouldn't want to lose it."

THE BED BY
THE WINDOW

The three old men shared a room at the nursing home.

Their room had only one window, but for them it was the only link to the real world. Ted Conklin, who had been there the longest, had the bed next to the window. When Ted died, the man in the next bed, George Best, took his place; and the third man, Richard Greene, took George's bed.

Despite his illness, George was a cheerful man who spent his days describing the sights he could see from his bed—pretty girls, a policeman on horseback, a traffic jam, a pizza parlor, a fire station and other scenes of life outside.

Richard loved to listen to George. But the more George talked about life outside, the more Richard wanted to *see* it for himself. Yet he knew that only when George died would he have his chance. He wanted to look out that window so badly that one day he decided to kill George. "He is going to die soon, anyway," he told himself. "What difference would it make?"

George had a bad heart. If he had an attack during the night and a nurse could not get to him right away, he had pills he could take. He kept them in a bottle on top of the cabinet between his bed and Richard's. All Richard had to do was knock the bottle to the floor where George could not reach it.

A few nights later George died just as Richard had planned he would. And the next morning Richard was moved to the bed by the window. Now he would see for himself all the things outside that

George had described.

After the nurses had left, Richard turned to the window and looked out. But all he could see was a blank brick wall.

THE DEAD
MAN'S HAND

The students at the school for nurses got along quite well with one another, except for Alice. The trouble with Alice was that she was perfect. At least that is how it seemed to the other students.

She was always friendly and always cheerful. Nothing ever upset her. Her school assignments were always on time, and always perfect. She didn't even bite her fingernails.

Many of the student nurses resented Alice. They would have liked to see her fail at something—become frightened, or cry, or do something that showed she had weaknesses like they did.

One night several students tried to frighten Alice with a practical joke. They borrowed the hand of a corpse they had been studying in anatomy and tied it to the light cord in her closet. When she tried to turn on the light, she would find herself holding a dead man's hand. "That would scare anybody," one of them said. "If it doesn't scare her, nothing will."

After tying the hand in place, they went to the movies. When they got back, Alice was asleep. But when they didn't see her the next morning, they decided to find out what had happened.

There was no sign of Alice in her room. But they soon found her. She was sitting on the floor in her closet staring at the dead man's hand and mumbling to herself. Alice didn't even look up.

The "joke" had worked, but nobody was laughing.

A GHOST IN
THE MIRROR

This is a scary game that young people sometimes play—trying to conjure up a ghost in their bathroom mirror. Many don't *really* believe that a ghost is going to appear. But they try to raise one anyway, for the fun and the excitement.

Some are willing to settle for any ghost, but others have a particular ghost in mind. One of these is a ghost named Mary Worth, who also is known as Mary Jane and Bloody Mary. She is the heroine of an old comic strip, but some say she actually was a witch who was hanged at the infamous witch trials in Salem, Massachusetts, in 1692.

Another of these ghosts is *"La Llorona,"* the weeping woman who wanders the streets of cities and towns from Texas to California and throughout Mexico, looking for her lost child.

Still another is Mary Whales, a young woman who is supposed to have been killed in a car accident in

Indianapolis, Indiana, about 1965. Her ghost is one of the "vanishing hitchhikers." It is said that again and again she thumbs a ride home in a passing car, then vanishes before she gets there.

Here is how ghost hunters try to raise a ghost:

1. They find a quiet bathroom, close the door, and turn off the lights.

2. While they stare at their face in the mirror, they repeat the ghost's name, usually forty-seven times or a hundred times. If any ghost will do, they say "any ghost" in place of a name. If they do manage to raise one, its face will slowly replace their face in the mirror.

Some say a ghost is likely to be angry at being disturbed. If it gets angry enough, they say, it will try to shatter the mirror and come right into the room. But a player can always turn on the lights and send the ghost back to where it came from. And when that happens, the game is over.

THE CURSE

My dad's friend, Charlie Potter, was a small, nervous man who was always looking around, as if he was in some kind of danger. After he told me this story about his college fraternity, I understood why.

"The frat doesn't exist anymore," he said. "It was banned years ago. We had just nine members at that point and were taking in two more: Jack Lawton and Ernie Kramer.

"One night in January, just about this time of year, the nine of us took them out into the country for their initiation. We took them to an old deserted house where two young men about our age had been murdered recently. Their murderer was still at large.

"We gave Jack a lighted candle and told him to go up to the third floor. 'Stay there for an hour,' we told him, 'then come back down. Don't speak. Don't make any noise. If your candle goes out, carry on in the dark.'

"From where we were standing, we could see the light from Jack's candle moving up the stairs to the second floor, then to the third. But when he got to the third floor, his candle went out.

"We guessed that he had come to a drafty corner, and the wind blew it out. But when the hour went by and he didn't come down, we weren't so sure. We waited another fifteen minutes and got more and more nervous.

"So we sent Ernie Kramer up after him. When Ernie got to the third floor, his candle also went out. We waited ten minutes, twenty minutes, but there was no sign of either of them. 'Come on down,' we called, but they didn't answer.

"Finally, we decided to go and get them. Armed

with flashlights, we started up the stairs. It was as quiet and dark as a grave in that house. When we got to the second floor, we called out again, but there was no answer.

"When we got to the third floor, we walked into a great big open space like an attic. Jack and Ernie weren't there. But we saw footprints in the dust. These led to a room on the other side of the attic.

"That room was also empty. But there was fresh blood on the floor, and the window was wide open. It was about twenty-five feet to the ground, but there was no ladder or rope in sight that they could have used to get down.

"We searched the rest of the house and the land around the house and found nothing. We decided that they were playing a trick on us. We figured that in some way they had escaped through the window and were hiding in the woods. The blood on the floor was to throw us off the track. We guessed that they'd show up the next day with a lot of stories and a lot of laughs. But they didn't.

"The next day we told the Dean of Men what had happened, and he reported it to the police. The police didn't find anything either, and after several weeks the search ended. To this day no one knows what happened to Jack Lawton and Ernie Kramer.

"There isn't much more to tell," he said. "We weren't arrested, but the college disbanded the fraternity and suspended the nine of us from school for a year.

"The strangest part came after we graduated. Someone must have placed a curse on us. Every year since then, around the time of that initiation, one of us has died or gone crazy.

"I'm the only one left," he said, "and I'm in pretty good health. But there are times when I feel just a little peculiar. . . ."

(Now rush at someone in the audience and SCREAM:)

AAAAAAAAAAH!

THE LAST LAUGH

These stories are scary and *funny.*

THE CHURCH

There was a fellow named Larry Berger who wasn't afraid of anybody alive. But anybody who was dead scared the wits out of him.

One night Larry was out driving in the country in his old jeep when he got caught in a bad thunderstorm. The rain was coming down in sheets. Since his jeep didn't have a top to it, Larry started looking for a place to take shelter.

But at the first place he came to he didn't even slow down. It was an old deserted cabin, probably as dry as a bone inside. But Larry knew for a fact that it was haunted, and he wasn't going to stay there.

A few miles farther, he came to an old abandoned church standing all alone in a field. It hadn't been used in years. All the window glass was gone, but it still had sections of the roof intact. So Larry parked his jeep and ran inside.

It was as dark as could be in there. Larry groped around until he found a pew and sat down. It was nice and dry, just as he had thought it would be, and he stretched out his legs and made himself comfortable.

Suddenly there was a big flash of lightning, and Larry saw that he wasn't the only one in that church. There were people sitting in almost every pew. They all had their heads bowed as if they were praying, and they all were dressed in white.

"These must be ghosts sitting in their shrouds," Larry thought. "They must have come in from some graveyard to get dry."

Larry jumped up and ran down the aisle as fast as he could, right smack into one of the ghosts. And the ghost, he went—BAA-A-A!

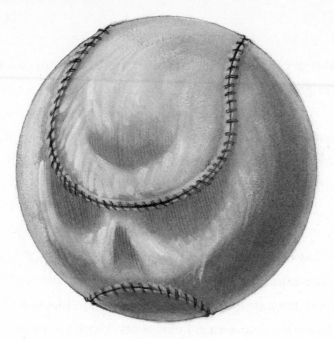

THE BAD NEWS

Leon and Todd loved baseball. When they were
young, they had played on the town's baseball team.
Leon had been the pitcher, and Todd had played second base. Now that they were a lot older, they spent
their free time watching baseball games on TV and
talking about baseball.

"Do you think they play baseball in Heaven?"
Leon asked Todd one day.

"That's a good question," said Todd. "The one

who gets there first should let the other one know somehow."

As it turned out, Todd got to Heaven first, and Leon waited patiently to hear from him. One day Leon found Todd sitting in the living room waiting for him.

Leon was very excited to see him. "What is it like up there?" he asked. "And what about baseball?"

"When it comes to baseball," said Todd, "I have some good news, and I have some bad news. The good news is that we do play baseball in Heaven. We have some fine teams. I play second base on my team, just like I used to in the old days. That's the good news."

"What's the bad news?" asked Leon.

"The bad news," said Todd, "is that you are scheduled to pitch tomorrow."

CEMETERY SOUP

On her way home from the market, the woman took a short cut through the cemetery. There, sticking up out of the ground, she saw a big bone. She picked it up and looked it over carefully.

"This will make a very good soup bone," she said. "I think I'll take it home. It's perfect weather for hot soup."

When she got home, the first thing she did was start the soup. Into the big soup pot went water, carrots, green beans, corn, barley, onions, potatoes, a snitch of beef, some salt and pepper, and—the bone. She brought it all to a boil, then brought it down to a simmer.

"Yum!" she said, sniffing it and tasting it. "I can hardly wait till supper."

Suddenly she heard a small voice.

"Please give me back my bone."

The woman paid no attention. Soon she heard the voice again.

"May I have back my bone, please?"

The woman was reading the newspaper, and again she didn't take any notice. In a little while, the voice spoke up once more. It was beginning to sound angry.

"Give me back my bone!"

The woman kept on reading the paper.

"Some people are too impatient," she muttered.

Once more the voice spoke. Now it sounded *very* angry, and it was so loud that the whole house shook.

"I WANT MY BONE BACK!"

The woman reached into the pot, grabbed the bone, and threw it out the window. In a voice just as loud, she shouted,

"TAKE IT!"

There was an eerie silence. Then the woman heard footsteps scurrying away from the house down the road toward the cemetery. And she got up and served herself some soup.

THE BROWN SUIT

A woman came to the funeral parlor to see her husband's corpse.

"You did a good job," she said to the undertaker. "He looks just the way he always looked, except for one thing. My husband always wore a brown suit, but you have him dressed in a blue suit."

"That is no problem," said the undertaker. "We can easily change it."

When she returned later, her husband was wearing a brown suit.

"Now he looks just the way he always did," she said. "I know you went to a lot of trouble."

"It was no trouble," he said. "As it happened, there is a man here who was wearing a brown suit, and his widow felt that blue would be better. He is about your husband's size. So we gave him the blue one and gave your husband the brown one."

"Even so," she said, "changing all that clothing was a big job."

"Not really," said the undertaker. "All we did was exchange their heads."

BA-ROOOM!

O'Leary is dead,
and O'Riley don't know it.
O'Riley is dead,
and O'Leary don't know it.
They both are dead
in the very same bed,
and neither one knows
that the other one's dead.
BA-ROOOM! BA-ROOOM!

To the tune of "The Irish Washerwoman"

THUMPITY-THUMP

When we moved to Schenectady from Schoharie, we rented a house awful cheap 'cause it was spooked, and nobody would live in it. But we didn't care, 'cause we didn't take no stock in spooks.

We had just gone to bed the first night, dog tired from riding in a wagon all day. We hadn't had time to shut our eyes when we heard a *thumpity-thump, thumpity-thump* comin' down the attic stairs. I covered my head with the blankets, but I couldn't shut out the sound. *Thumpity-thump, thumpity-thump*, it went. I could hear it plain as day.

Past the bedroom door *thumpity-thump, thumpity-thump* and down the stairs *thumpity-thump, thumpity-thump* and through the kitchen *thumpity-thump, thumpity-thump* and down the cellar stairs *thumpity-thump, thumpity-thump*, makin' the most awful racket you ever heard. It was more than we could stand. So we all followed the sound to see what was goin' on.

When we got down the cellar stairs, we saw that it was a chair that had made all of that racket. There it was, with one of its legs pointin' to a place on the dirt floor. We all just stood and gawped till my brother Ike said that he believed that the chair was trying to tell us something about the place it was pointing at.

So Ike went and got a shovel and started diggin'. He didn't have to dig far before his shovel struck somethin' hard. Pretty soon we could see the edge of a box stickin' out. We all hollered for him to hurry up and uncover the rest of it. And the chair—it got so excited, it jumped up and down like it had gone plumb crazy.

When Ike got the box uncovered, Pop and the boys pried off the lid. And there was the body of a man all smooched with blood. It was plain as the nose on your face that he had been murdered, and the chair wanted folks to know it. Right then and there we decided to leave. Bein' strangers, everybody would think that we had murdered him and come there to hide the body. It didn't take us long to fill up that hole and get out of that house.

The chair was awful mad about our leavin', and it went up the cellar stairs *thumpity-thump, thumpity-thump* louder than when it had gone down. Then it *thumpity-thump*ed up the next set of stairs and the next louder still. When it got back into the attic, it *THUMPITY-THUMP*ED so loud we thought it would thump all the plasterin' down on our heads.

Nobody asked us why we were movin' out so soon, 'cause nobody ever stayed more than one night in that place, and most not that long. But I can tell you we were thankful to get back to Schoharie where chairs stay where they're put and don't go rarin' and rampagin' 'roun, scarin' folks out of their wits, pointin' out murders and goodness knows what!

ABBREVIATIONS IN NOTES, SOURCES, AND BIBLIOGRAPHY

AF	*Arkansas Folklore*
CFQ	*California Folklore Quarterly*
HF	*Hoosier Folklore*
HFB	*Hoosier Folklore Bulletin*
IF	*Indiana Folklore*
IUFA	Indiana University Folklore Archive, Bloomington, Ind.
JAF	*Journal of American Folklore*
KFQ	*Kentucky Folklore Quarterly*
NEFA	Northeast Archives of Folklore and Oral History, University of Maine, Orono, Me.
PTFS	Publication of the Texas Folklore Society
SFQ	*Southern Folklore Quarterly*
SS	Alvin Schwartz, *Scary Stories to Tell in the Dark*
WF	*Western Folklore*

NOTES

The publications cited are described in the Bibliography.

Hoo-Ha's (Introduction): The term "heebie-jeebies" comes from a pre-World War I comic-strip cartoonist named W. DeBeck. The term "screaming meemies" was the name first given to the whistling shells that the German army fired at the Allies during World War I. Various dictionaries.

Living Ghosts (Chapter 1): There has always been a belief that the dead can return to our world in ghost form, if they have a need to do so. They may be invisible, or rise up like a drifting mist, or appear as they did when they were alive. Of these living ghosts, the best known are the ghostly or vanishing hitchhikers. There are many tales about them. Usually there is a main character who dies, then makes repeated efforts to return home or to familiar surroundings. The ghost manages to hitchhike a ride in a passing car, but always vanishes just before the car reaches its destination. There are several tales of living ghosts in Chapter 1: "Something Was Wrong," "The Wreck," and "One Sunday Morning." For a detailed discussion of ghosts, see *SS*, pp. 90–92.

"One Sunday Morning" (p. 9): This tale is rooted in

the ancient belief that the night belongs to the dead and that places of worship are haunted after dark.

The scholar Alexander Krappe suggested that it may also be rooted in a dream, possibly in an experience in which the dreamer walked in her sleep. It might be, he said, that the dreamer actually walked to the site of the dream and continued dreaming until she awakened, and in that way provided a basis for a tale. What if she found on awakening, as Ida did, that her clothes had been torn or that she had suffered a bad scratch? Such things could be explained in a number of ways, he said.

Krappe told of a German physician in the nineteenth century. When he was in high school, the physician lived in the same house with a seventeen-year-old boy who walked in his sleep. One night the boy dreamed that it was seven o'clock in the morning and time to go to school.

While still asleep, he washed, dressed, got his books together, and went downstairs. On his way out the door, he stopped to check the time, as he did every morning. Just then the clock struck midnight, chiming twelve times, and awakened him.

Had the boy not awakened, Krappe suggested that he probably would have gone to school, just as Ida in "One Sunday Morning" went to church where she continued to dream. See Krappe, *Balor*, pp. 114–25; *JAF* 60: pp. 159–62.

"Sounds" (p. 12): The person who found this legend was a newspaperman from Brooklyn, NY, named Charles M. Skinner. Although not a trained folklorist, Skinner was the first serious collector of American legends. Between 1896 and 1903 he compiled five books of legends from throughout the United States and its possessions, some of which became bestsellers. In all, Skinner found and retold

515 legends dealing with ghosts, treasures, Indian uprisings, witches, rescues, and other subjects. Only in recent years have folklorists become interested in such material. See Dorson, "Skinner."

"Somebody Fell from Aloft" (p. 17): A writer and artist named George S. Wasson was the author of this tale and others that suggested the kinds of stories being told in Maine fishing villages during the nineteenth century. They were based on his knowledge of the local tales and dialects in such places. All involved a small port named Killick Cove, actually Kittery Point in southern Maine, where Wasson lived. See Dorson, Jonathan, pp. 243–48.

"Clinkity-Clink" (p. 26): This is one of the famous Uncle Remus stories that Joel Chandler Harris created from Negrotales, songs, customs, and ways of speaking he learned as a white boy in the Old South.

His stories on Negro plantation life first appeared in 1878 in the newspaper *The Atlanta Constitution*. The first of his books, *Uncle Remus: His Songs and Sayings*, appeared two years later and brought him fame. Nine other collections followed, including *Uncle Remus and Brer Rabbit* and *The Tar Baby and Other Rhymes of Uncle Remus*.

They evoked a remarkable sense of the life and character of the Negro in the Old South, with Uncle Remus serving the traditional role of an elderly Negro, storyteller to the master's children. See Brookes, pp. 3–21; 43–62.

Buried Alive (p. 35, "Rings on Her Fingers"): When a dead person is embalmed, a fluid commonly containing formaldehyde is pumped into the blood and lymph systems. It preserves the body for a long time. It also assures that the person who is being buried is dead.

Before modern methods of embalming became widespread, there were many legends like "Rings on Her Fingers." Each told of how some person had been given up for dead when actually they were in a coma or trance of some kind, and regained consciousness during their funeral or after they had been buried. In the latter case, those who were rescued from a horrible death owed their lives to grave robbers.

In those years thieves dug up corpses for their jewels, or they stole the corpses and sold them to medical schools. Now and then they found a living person who was revived by the shock of cold air or by the efforts they were making to cut off one of their fingers. See Sources for "Rings."

In the early 1800s an English woman was so concerned about being buried alive, she arranged to be buried in a funeral vault in a coffin without a lid. A small opening was left in the wall of the vault so that she could breathe and be heard if she regained consciousness. See Hole, p. 54.

Vampires (p. 44): The vampire in the tale "The Window" is a living corpse, a person who died but is not always dead. It cannot rest in its grave. It spends each night searching for a human from whose throat it can suck the blood it needs. But by cockcrow it must return to its coffin.

People in many parts of the world believe in vampires. But the belief is strongest and most widespread in Russia, Poland, Romania, Bulgaria, Hungary, and Greece. In eighteenth-century Hungary, the outcry over the threat of vampires was as great as the concern over witches in New England a hundred years earlier.

There are few detailed accounts of vampire experiences in America or the British Isles. One is a brief tale collected in 1933 in Crane, Missouri, by Vance Randolph. It tells of a boy who went into a witch's yard to retrieve a ball he had been playing with. The witch's daughter cut his throat and, with her mother, drank his blood. Randolph suggests that it is related to the ballad "Sir Hugh," which involves a similar incident.

The English story "The Window" is probably one of the most detailed of the English-language accounts. However, the description of the method used to destroy the vampire may not have been complete. In the Eastern European tradition, the vampire would have been decapitated before it was cremated. Then its remains would have been buried at a crossroads. There also is one other traditional method of ensuring the vampire will not return: driving a sharpened wooden stake through the vampire's heart.

It is said that only certain people become vampires: witches, suicides, and persons who were bitten by a vampire. If a corpse is buried with its mouth open or a cat jumps over the corpse while it is being buried, the corpse will also become a vampire.

It is said that the best way to ward off a vampire is to wear bells, garlic, or iron in some form.

See Leach, *Dictionary*, p. 1154; Randolph, *Church House*, pp. 164–65; *Ozark Folksongs*, vol. 1, pp. 148–51; Belden, pp. 69–73.

Horror Stories (p. 57, "Oh, Susannah!"): This is one of a group of unusually popular legends about atrocities committed by mad killers at loose on or near college campuses. They include stories of young people who have been struck with an ax or stabbed with a knife, whose cries for help are ignored because their roommates are too frightened to open the door to their room. The folklorist Linda Dégh suggests that these legends are modern cautionary tales warning young people of the dangers that threaten them as they are increasingly on their own. See Barnes, 307–12; Dégh, "The Roommate's Death," *IF* 2; *SS*, 95–96.

Poltergeists (p. 87, "Thumpity-Thump"): The haunted chair in this story is a poltergeist, a term that means literally "noise ghost." However, such a ghost usually is invisible. It makes its presence known through knocking and rapping sounds and other noises and actions for which there is no explanation.

Such ghosts are said to move furniture, cause dishes to fly from cupboards and crash to the floor, hurl burning chunks of wood from fireplaces, and even cut clothing and blankets into strange shapes, often crescents, with invisible shears. See Gardner, pp. 96–97; Musick, *West Virginia*, p. 42; Lawson and Porter, 371–82.

In *Pickwick Papers*, Dickens tells of a talking chair that helps a traveling salesman win the hand of the woman he wants to marry. See Dickens, pp. 188–96.

SOURCES

The sources of each item are given, along with variants and related information. When available, names of collectors (C) and informants (I) are given. The publications cited are described in the Bibliography.

Introduction

p. xi   *Hoo-Ha's*: From a T. S. Eliot poem, "Fragment of an Agon." See Eliot, p. 84.

When She Saw Him, She Screamed and Ran

p. 3   *"Something Was Wrong"*: Retelling of an untitled story in Cerf, *Try and Stop Me*, pp. 275–76.

   p. 5   *"The Wreck"*: Based on a brief reference in Parochetti, 55. This is one of the many "ghostly hitchhiker" stories in which a young woman is given a ride home in a car, then turns out to be a ghost. See Beardsley, Richard K., *CFQ* 1: 303–36; *CFQ* 2: 3–25; *SS*: p. 121. See the Note "Living Ghosts."

   p. 9   *"One Sunday Morning"*: I first heard this tale as a student at Northwestern University, Evanston, 111., in the 1950s. The text is based on my recollections, but also on references in Krappe, *Balor*, pp. 114–25, and Krappe,

JAF 60: 159–62. See the Note "One Sunday Morning."

p. 12   *"Sounds"*: Based on a legend in Mobile, Alabama, toward the end of the nineteenth century. The deserted house described in the text was built by a wealthy Englishman who lived there with his daughter, who he said was "half-witted," and several servants. No one visited them, and they seldom went out. He abruptly returned to England without her. She disappeared. The house was sold again and again. No one could live there. See Skinner, pp. 17–19. See the Note "Sounds."

p. 15   *"A Weird Blue Light"*: Retold from a newspaper report in the Downey, Cal., *Champion*, Dec. 17, 1892, taken from the Galveston, Tex., *True Flag*, n.d., reprinted in Splitter, p. 209.

p. 17   *"Somebody Fell from Aloft"*: Adapted and abridged from a story in Wasson, "Who Fell from Aloft?", pp. 106–28. See the Note "Somebody Fell from Aloft."

p. 23   *"The Little Black Dog"*: This tale of a dog seeking revenge is adapted from the Ozark Mountains story "Si Burton's Little Black Dog," (I): Mrs. Marie Wilbur, Pineville, Mo., 1929. See Randolph, *Church House*, pp. 171–73.

p. 26   *"Clinkity-Clink"*: A late-nineteenth-century Southern Negro version of the well-known jump story "The Golden Arm," in which a golden arm or some other part of the body is stolen from a corpse who returns from the grave to claim it. It is adapted from Harris, "A Ghost Story," *Nights with Uncle Remus*, pp. 164–69. See the Note "Clinkity-Clink."

She Was Spittin' and Yowlin' Just Like a Cat

p. 33 *"The Bride"*: Retelling of a traditional English and American tale, based on variants and the lyrics of the ballad "The Mistletoe Bough" by the songwriter Thomas Haynes Bayly. This is the last verse:

> At length an oak chest that had long lain hid,
> Was found in the castle; they raised the lid,
> And a skeleton form lay mouldering there
> In the bridal wreath of the lady fair.
> Oh, sad was her fate; in sporting jest
> She hid from her lord in the old oak chest;
> It closed with a spring, and her bridal bloom
> Lay withering there in a living tomb.

There was even a play about the unfortunate bride, "The Mistletoe Bough; or the Fatal Chest" by Charles A. Somerset. See Briggs and Tongue, pp. 88; Disher, pp. 89–90.

p. 35 *"Rings on Her Fingers"*: Retold from several variants. Dorson, *Buying the Wind*, pp. 310–11; Baylor, "Folklore from Socorro, New Mexico," pp. 100–102. The conclusion in which the grave robber dies was suggested by the fate of "The Thievish Sexton," Briggs and Tongue, pp. 88–89. See the Note "Buried Alive."

p. 39 *"The Drum"*: Cautionary tales warning children to behave or suffer the consequences are found in most cultures. "The Drum" is a retelling of such a story which was passed down by several generations of an English family, then migrated to America with another family member. In the retelling in this book, the title has been shortened from "The Pear Drum," and the names of the children have been changed from "Blue-Eyes" and "Turkey" to "Dolores" and "Sandra." See the text and letter from J. Y. Bell and the letter from Lilian H. Hayward, in which she recalls a literary version of such a story that appeared in England during the late nineteenth century, *Folklore* 66 (1955): 302–4, 431.

The folklorist Katharine M. Briggs regards the gypsy girl in the story as a kind of Satan in offering the drum in return for evil behavior, but as more evil; for the girl goes back on her bargain, something Satan would not do. Briggs, Part A, Vol. 2, pp. 554–55.

p. 44   *"The Window"*: Adapted and abridged from Hare, pp. 50–52. See the Note "Vampires."

p. 49   *"Wonderful Sausage"*: Retold from several variants and a song. See Randolph, "The Bloody Miller," *Turtle*, pp. 138–40, (I): Mrs. Elizabeth Maddocks, Joplin, Mo., 1937; Edwards, p. 8, an Arkansas variant; and Saxon, p. 258, a New Orleans legend in which a sausage maker grinds his wife into sausage and is driven mad by her ghost.

The song is entitled "Donderback's Machine," or just "Donderback," with various spellings, and minor variations. It concludes when Donderback's sausage grinder breaks down, and he climbs inside to repair it:

His wife she had the nightmare,
She walked right in her sleep,
She grabbed the crank, gave it a yank,
and Donderback was meat.

It is sung to the tune of "The Son of a Gambolier,"

which became the tune for "I'm a Ramblin' Wreck from Georgia Tech." See Spaeth, p. 90; Randolph, *Ozark Folksongs*, vol. 3, pp. 488–89.

p. 51 *"The Cat's Paw"*: Retold from a widespread witch tale. See Randolph, *Ozark Mountain Folks*, p. 37; Randolph, "The Cat's Foot," *Turtle*, pp. 174–75, (I): Lon Jordon, Farmington, Ark., 1941; Puckett, p. 149; Gardner, p. 174; Porter, p. 115.

p. 53 *"The Voice"*: Traditional jump story, to which the compiler added the two concluding lines. See *SS*, p. 7, p. 14; Opie, p. 36; Saxon, p. 277.

When I Wake Up, Everything Will Be All Right

p. 57 *"Oh, Susannah!"*: A well-known legend among college students, this frequently is entitled "The Roommate's Death." The text in this book is retold from a number of variants: NEFA, (I): Linda Mansfield, (C): Mary Dudley, Orono, Me., 1964; IUFA, (I): Shelly Herbst, (C): Diane Pavy, Bloomington, Ind., 1960; questionnaire interview by the compiler with Lin Rogove, Lancaster, Pa., 1982; *IF* 3 (1970): 67. See the Note "Horror Stories."

p. 59 *"The Man in the Middle"*: This legend has been told in New York, London, Paris, and other big cities with subways. Around the turn of the century the same story was being told about a horse car, a horse-drawn bus in New York as it moved south on Fifth Avenue in a snowstorm. See "Folklore in the News": *WF* 8: 174; Clough, pp. 355–56.

p. 61 *"The Cat in a Shopping Bag"*: I first heard this story in the late 1970s in Denver and Helena, Montana. Text is based on my recollections and similar versions in

Brunvand, pp. 108–9, collected in the Salt Lake City area in 1975.

p. 63   *"The Bed by the Window"*: Retold from Cerf, *Try and Stop Me*, pp. 288–89.

p. 66   *"The Dead Man's Hand"*: A tale told in medical and nursing schools. Retold from variants in Parochetti, p. 53, and Baughman, "The Cadaver Arm," pp. 30–32. In another variant, the victim is found dead with the dead man's hand clutching his throat, Barnes, p. 307.

p. 68   *"A Ghost in the Mirror"*: Based on references in Knapp, p. 242; Langlois, pp. 196–204; Perez, pp. 73–74, 76.

p. 70   *"The Curse"*: A retelling of a legend frequently entitled "The Fatal Fraternity Initiation." It is based on several variants: Baughman, "The Fatal Initiation," *HFB* 4: 49–55; NEFA, (I): Linette Bridges, (C): Patricia J. Curtis, Blue Hill, Me., 1967; Dégh, *Indiana Folklore: A Reader*, pp. 159–60.

The Last Laugh

p. 77   *"The Church"*: Retold from a text in Randolph, *Sticks*, pp. 24–25, (I): Wayne Hogue, Memphis, Tenn., 1952.

p. 79   *"The Bad News"*: (I): Constance Paras, 12, Winchester-Thurston School, Pittsburgh, 1983.

p. 81   *"Cemetery Soup"*: This jump story is based on a tale in Puckett, pp. 124–25, (I): Marie Sneed, Burton, S.C., about 1925. For a similar English version, see Gilchrist, pp. 378–79.

p. 84   *"The Brown Suit"*: Compiler's recollection.

p. 86   *"BA-ROOOM!"*: Lyrics, (I): Margaret Z. Fisher. Manheim Township, Pa., 1982. Music, "The Irish

Washerwoman," a traditional dance tune played in fast jig time. Musical notation transcribed by Barbara C. Schwartz, Princeton, N.J., 1984, from a performance on the dulcimer by Thomas Mann, Ortonville, Iowa, 1937, tape recorded by Mrs. Sidney R. Cowell, in the recording "Folk Music of the United States, Play and Dance Songs and Tunes," ed., B. A. Botkin, Library of Congress Music Division, AAFSL9.

p. 87   *"Thumpity-Thump"*: Adapted from Gardner, pp. 96–97, (I): Maggie Zee, Middleburgh, N.Y., about 1914. See the Note "Poltergeists."

BIBLIOGRAPHY

Books

Books that may be of interest to young people are marked with an asterisk (*).

Baker, Ronald L. *Hoosier Folk Legends*. Bloomington, Ind.: Indiana University Press, 1982.

Belden, Henry M. *Ballads and Songs Collected by the Missouri Folklore Society*, vol. 15. Columbia, Mo.: University of Missouri, 1940.

Bennett, John. *The Doctor to the Dead: Grotesque Legends & Folk Tales of Old Charleston*. New York: Rinehart & Co., 1943.

Botkin, Benjamin A., ed. *A Treasury of American Folklore*. New York: Crown Publishers, 1944.

_____, ed. *A Treasury of New England Folklore*. New York: Crown Publishers, Inc., 1965.

Briggs, Katharine M. *A Dictionary of British Folktales*. 4 vols. Bloomington, Ind.: Indiana University Press, 1967.

Briggs, Katharine M., and Ruth L. Tongue. *Folktales of England*. Chicago, Ill.: University of Chicago Press, 1965.

Brookes, Stella B. *Joel Chandler Harris—Folklorist,*

Athens, Ga.: University of Georgia Press, 1950.

Brunvand, Jan H. *The Vanishing Hitchhiker: American Urban Legends and Their Meanings.* New York: W. W. Norton & Co., 1981.

*Cerf, Bennett A. *Famous Ghost Stories.* New York: Random House, 1944.

———. *Try and Stop Me.* New York: Simon and Schuster, 1944. Reprint Edition: Garden City, N.Y.: Garden City Books, 1954.

Clough, Ben C., ed. *The American Imagination at Work: Tall Tales and Folk Tales.* New York: Alfred A. Knopf, 1947.

Dégh, Linda. "The 'Belief Legend' in Modern Society: Form, Function and Relationship to Other Genres." In Wayland D. Hand, ed. *American Folk Legend, A Symposium.* Berkeley, Cal.: University of California Press, 1971.

———, ed. *Indiana Folklore: A Reader.* Bloomington, Ind.: University of Indiana Press, 1980.

Dickens, Charles. *Pickwick Papers: The Posthumous Papers of the Pickwick Club.* New York: The Heritage Press, 1938.

Disher, Maurice W. *Victorian Song: From Dive to Drawing Room.* London: Phoenix House, 1955.

Dorson, Richard M. *American Folklore.* Chicago, Ill.: University of Chicago Press, 1959.

———. "How Shall We Rewrite Charles M. Skinner Today?" In Wayland D. Hand, ed. *American Folk Legend, A Symposium.* Berkeley, Cal.: University of California Press, 1971.

———. *Jonathan Draws the Long Bow.* Cambridge, Mass.: Harvard University Press, 1946.

———, ed. *Bloodstoppers and Bearwalkers.* Cambridge, Mass.: Harvard University Press, 1952.

_____, ed. *Buying the Wind*. Chicago: University of Chicago Press, 1964.

_____, ed. *Negro Tales from Calvin, Michigan*. Bloomington, Ind.: Indiana University Press, 1958.

Eliot, T. S. *The Complete Poems and Plays, 1909–1950*. New York: Harcourt, Brace & World, 1952.

Gardner, Emelyn E. *Folklore from the Schoharie Hills, New York*. Ann Arbor, Mich.: University of Michigan Press, 1937.

Hare, Augustus, J. C. *The Story of My Life*. London: George Allen & Unwin, Ltd., 1950. An abridgement of Vols. 4, 5, and 6 of *The Story of My Life*, George Allen, 1900.

Harris, Joel Chandler. *Nights with Uncle Remus: Myths and Legends of the Old Plantation*. Boston: James R. Osgood & Co., 1882.

_____. Richard Chase, ed. *The Complete Tales of Uncle Remus*. Boston: Houghton Mifflin Company, 1955.

Hole, Christina. *Haunted England: A Survey of English Ghost-Lore*. London: B. T. Batsford, 1950.

Janvier, Thomas A. *Legends of the City of Mexico*. New York: Harper & Brothers, 1910.

*Jones, Louis C. *Things That Go Bump in the Night*. New York: Hill and Wang, 1959.

Knapp, Mary and Herbert. *One Potato, Two Potato: The Secret Education of American Children*. New York: W. W. Norton & Co., 1976.

Krappe, Alexander H. *Balor with the Evil Eye: Studies in Celtic and French Literature*. New York: *Institut des Études Françaises*, Columbia University, 1927.

Langlois, Janet. "Mary Whales, I Believe in You" in Linda Dégh, ed., *Indiana Folklore: A Reader*. See Dégh above.

*Leach, Maria. *Rainbow Book of American Folk Tales*

and Legends. Cleveland and New York: World Publishing Co., 1959.

*———. *The Thing at the Foot of the Bed and Other Scary Stories*. Cleveland and New York: World Publishing Co., 1959.

*———. *Whistle in the Graveyard*. New York: The Viking Press, 1974.

———, ed. *Standard Dictionary of Folklore, Mythology and Legend*. New York: Funk & Wagnalls Publishing Co., 1972.

Musick, Ruth Ann. *Riddles, Folk Songs and Folk Tales from West Virginia*. Morgantown, W. Va.: West Virginia University Library, 1960.

Opie, Iona and Peter. *The Lore and Language of Schoolchildren*. London: Oxford University Press, 1959.

Puckett, Newbell N. *Folk Beliefs of the Southern Negro*. Chapel Hill, N. C.: University of North Carolina Press, 1926.

Randolph, Vance. *From an Ozark Holler: Stories of Ozark Mountain Folk*. New York: The Vanguard Press, 1933.

———. *Ozark Mountain Folks*. New York: The Vanguard Press, 1932.

———. *Ozark Superstitions*. New York: Columbia University Press, 1947. Reprint edition: *Ozark Magic and Folklore*. New York: Dover Publications, 1964.

———. "Witches, and Witch-Masters." In Benjamin A. Botkin, ed. *Folk-Say: A Regional Miscellany*. Norman, Okla.: University of Oklahoma Press, 1931.

———, ed. *Ozark Folksongs*, vols. 1, 3. Columbia, Mo.: State Society of Missouri, 1949.

———, ed. *Sticks in the Knapsack and Other Ozark Folk Tales*. New York: Columbia University Press, 1958.

———, ed. *The Talking Turtle and Other Ozark Folk*

Tales. New York: Columbia University Press, 1957.

———, ed. *Who Blowed Up the Church House? And Other Ozark Folk Tales*. New York: Columbia University Press, 1952.

Saxon, Lyle *et al*. Louisiana Writers Project. *Gumbo Ya-Ya*. Boston: Houghton Mifflin Company, 1945.

*Schwartz, Alvin. *Scary Stories to Tell in the Dark*. New York: J. B. Lippincott, 1981.

Skinner, Charles M. *American Myths and Legends*. Vol. 2, Philadelphia: J. B. Lippincott Co., 1903.

Spaeth, Sigmund. *Read 'em and Weep, the Songs You Forgot to Remember*. Garden City, N.Y.: Doubleday, Page & Company, 1927.

Wasson, George S. *Captain Simeon's Store*. Boston: Houghton Mifflin Company, 1903.

Wilson, Charles M. "Folk Beliefs in the Ozark Hills." In Benjamin A. Botkin, ed. *Folk-Say: A Regional Miscellany*. Norman, Okla.: University of Oklahoma Press, 1930.

Articles

Bacon, A. M., and Parsons, E. C. "Folk-Lore from Elizabeth City County, Va.": *JAF* 35 (1922): 250–327.

Barnes, Daniel R. "Some Functional Horror Stories on the Kansas University Campus." *SFQ* 30 (1966): 305–12.

Baughman, Ernest. "The Cadaver Arm." *HFB* 4 (1945): 30–32.

———. "The Fatal Initiation." *HFB* 4 (1945): 49–55.

Baylor, Dorothy J. "Buried Alive Stories, Folklore from Socorro, New Mexico, Part II." *HF* 6 (1947): 100–102.

Beardsley, Richard K., and Hankey, Rosalie. "The History of the Vanishing Hitchhiker." *CFQ* 2 (1943): 3–25.

————. "The Vanishing Hitchhiker": *CFQ* 1 (1942): 303–36.

Bell, J. Y. "The Pear Drum." *Folklore* 66 (1955): 302–4.

Boggs, Ralph Steele. "North Carolina White Folktales and Riddles." *JAF* 47 (1934): 3–25.

Dégh, Linda. "The Hook, the Boyfriend's Death, and the Killer in the Back Seat." *IF* 1 (1968): 98–106.

————. "The Roomate's Death and Related Dormitory Stories in Formation." *IF* 2 (1969): 55–74.

Dorson, Richard M. "The Folklore of Colleges." *The American Mercury* 68 (1949): 671–77.

————. "Polish Tales from Joe Woods." *WF* 8 (1949): 131–45.

Edwards, J. C. "Dunderbeck." *AF* 2 (1952): 8.

Fauset, Arthur Huff. "Tales and Riddles Collected in Philadelphia." *JAF* 41 (1928): 529–57.

"Folk Tales, Folklore in the News." *WF* 8 (1949): 174–75.

Gilchrist, A. G. "The Bone." *Folklore* 50 (1939): 378–79.

Grider, Sylvia. "Dormitory Legend-Telling in Process." *IF* 6 (1973): 1–32.

Hawes, Bess Lomax. "*La Llorona* in Juvenile Hall." *WF* 27: 153–70.

Hayward, Lilian H. "Correspondence." *Folklore* 66 (1955): 431.

Krappe, Alexander H. "The Spectres' Mass." *JAF* 60 (1947): 159–62.

Lawson, O. G., and Porter, Kenneth W. "Texas Poltergeist, 1881." *JAF* 64 (1951): 371–82.

Leddy, Betty. "*La Llorona* in Southern Arizona." *WF* 7 (1948): 272–77.

Parochetti, JoAnn S. "Scary Stories from Purdue." *KFQ* 10 (1965): 49–57.

Perez, Soledad. "Mexican Folklore from Austin, Texas." PTFS 24 (1951): 71–136.

Porter, F. Hampden. "Notes on the Folk-Lore of the Mountain Whites of the Alleghenies." *JAF* 7 (1894): 105–17.

Splitter, Henry W. "New Tales of American Phantom Ships." *WF* 9 (1950): 201–16.

ACKNOWLEDGMENTS

I am grateful to the girls and boys in many parts of the country who have shared with me their scary stories and told me about stories they would like to see in collections of this kind.

I am also grateful to the following persons and organizations for their generous help:

The librarians and library staff at the University of Maine (Orono), the University of Pennsylvania, Princeton University, and the Princeton, N.J., Public Library; Professor Edward D. Ives of the University of Maine and Professor Kenneth Goldstein of the University of Pennsylvania; my editors, Nina Ignatowicz and Robert O. Warren; and my wife and colleague, Barbara Carmer Schwartz.

—A. S.